T0346567

Spinning Tails

WRITTEN BY TOM KNISELY

ILLUSTRATED BY MEGAN LLOYD

STACKPOLE
BOOKS

Guilford, Connecticut

To my grandchildren, Windsor, Imogen, Jai, and Bodhi. –*Tom*

For the Kauffmans and the Deans, keepers of the barn.
Thank you for sharing this special place with me. –*Love, M L-T*

Published by Stackpole Books
An imprint of Globe Pequot, the trade division of The Rowman & Littlefield Publishing Group, Inc.
4501 Forbes Blvd., Ste. 200
Lanham, MD 20706
www.stackpolebooks.com

Distributed by NATIONAL BOOK NETWORK
800-462-6420

Text Copyright © 2021 Tom Knisely
Illustrations Copyright © 2021 Megan Lloyd-Thompson

British Library Cataloguing in Publication Information available

Library of Congress Cataloging-in-Publication Data available

ISBN 978-0-8117-3914-6 (cloth : alk. paper)
ISBN 978-0-8117-6904-4 (electronic)

∞™ The paper used in this publication meets the minimum requirements of American National Standard for Information Sciences—Permanence of Paper for Printed Library Materials, ANSI/NISO Z39.48-1992.

In an old weathered barn filled with hay and wildflowers
live five fat sheep and a family of mice.

In winter they live in the cottage next door, where an old
man weaves rugs on a loom. The mice help the weaver with
his work and sleep in a soft rag rug, toasty and warm.
But in spring they move to the barn and make a nest in the hay.

It's a bit scratchy and a bit itchy, but the hay smells sweet, there is plenty of grain to eat, and they like to listen to the sheep down below in their stall.

BAA. BAAA. BAAAAAAA!

Early one morning, the mice heard a new sound.

CLIP. CLIP. CLIP!
BAA. BAAA. BAAAAA!

BAA. CLIP.
BAAA. CLIP.

BAAA. BAAAA. CLIP!

"What's that?" asked a curious mouse.
"It's shearing day," said Father Mouse, "when the weaver clips the wool off the sheep so they'll be cooler in the summer."

"And so he'll have wool to spin into yarn," said Mother Mouse.

Peering down from the loft, the mice watched as the weaver
rolled each sheep onto its backside, belly facing skyward.
He took some funny-looking scissors and began to clip.
"They're getting a haircut!" squeaked one small mouse.

As the weaver worked, the fat, round sheep started to look
smaller and skinnier, until, finally, all their fluffy wool
was piled up beside them. The mice giggled at the
sight of the nearly naked sheep.

"They won't be naked for long," said Mother Mouse.
"Their wool will grow back and by winter they'll
be toasty warm in fluffy new coats."

The mice watched as the weaver thanked the sheep for their fleece, gathered the wool in a sheet, and carried it to the cottage yard, where three large pots stood. One was filled with hot, soapy water. Two were filled with clean hot water, and one of these was hung over a small fire. The weaver gently pushed the wool down into the sudsy pot to soak.

He returned to the barn, climbed the ladder to the loft, and gathered some of the wildflowers hanging from the rafters.

"This goldenrod will dye that white wool a beautiful yellow, perfect for the yarn I want to spin. I want to weave a blanket for the woman who gave me these fine, fat sheep, and yellow is her favorite color," said the weaver.

Back in the cottage yard, the weaver put the goldenrod
into the kettle hanging over the fire. He carefully removed
the wool from the soapy kettle and put it into the kettle of
clean water to rinse.

Finally, he gently moved the wool to the steaming kettle
of goldenrod. The water in that kettle was now a lovely
yellow!

The white wool slowly turned golden. When it was just the color the weaver wanted, he carefully removed it from the pot, squeezed out the water, and scattered the wool on bushes to dry in the sun.

"Oh, look at my nice, yellow wool!" said the weaver.

The next day, the mice watched the weaver pick pieces of hay and dirt out of the wool and use hand carders to brush the wool into fluffy tufts. Then he sat in the cottage yard to spin.

WHIR, WHIR, WHIR

went his spindle as he twisted the wool into yarn.

"How does he DO that?" asked one of the mice. "It almost makes me dizzy," squeaked another.

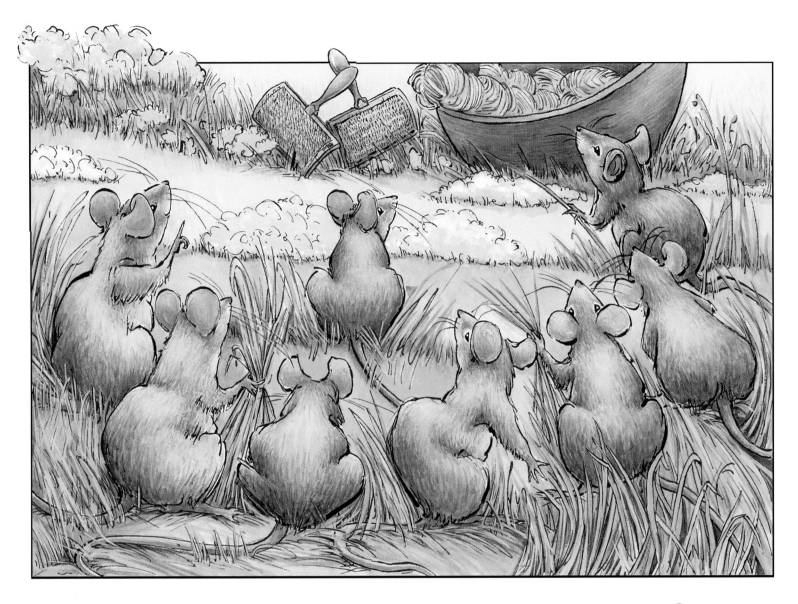

"Look at all that fluffy wool," said a third. "It would make a nice, soft bed to sleep in—so much better than our scratchy hay bed. Do you think the weaver would mind if we took some?"

"Well," said Father Mouse, "I suppose we could each take just a little."

That night, while the weaver slept, the mice crept down
to the yard. Each took a paw-full of fluffy, yellow wool.
One or two mice took very large paw-fulls. Three or
four mice snuck back for more.

By morning, the mice had
turned their hay nest into a
fluffy, yellow bed of wool.

Down in the yard, the weaver
emerged from his cottage,
yawning and stretching.
He gathered up the remaining
wool to spin.

WHIR, WHIR, WHIR

WHIR, WHIR, WHIR

When he finished spinning, he dressed his loom and began
to weave. By evening he was almost done with his blanket,
but he was also out of yarn!

"I was sure I had enough wool for this blanket," he said to himself. "I had a lot of fleece.
NOW what am I going to do? My friend is coming tomorrow to get her blanket but I can't finish it. I'll have to call her in the morning and tell her not to come."

Puzzled, tired, and disappointed, the weaver climbed the stairs and fell into bed.

"Did you hear that?" asked Mother Mouse. "The weaver needs the wool we took for our beds."
"And he needs it to be spun into yarn by tomorrow," said Father Mouse.

"I think we can help," said the littlest mouse. "We were watching him all day and I think we could spin our fleece into yarn."

"But we can't use his big spindle," said another mouse.

"Wait here," said Father Mouse, "I have an idea."

Father Mouse scampered
into the cottage and
up the stairs to the
weaver's bedroom.
Quietly, quietly,
he chewed and chewed.

Back down the stairs he went, stopping to climb the counter for something else to help them spin. Then it was outside to his waiting family, and off they all went, back to the barn.

"These toothpicks and buttons make perfect spindles," cried Mother Mouse as the family spun and spun and spun their lovely yellow wool.

The next morning, the weaver was surprised to find every other button on his shirt was missing. He could only button his suspenders at one spot, which made his pants hang down at a dangerous angle!

"What happened to my clothes?"

He almost tripped going downstairs where, to his amazement, he saw eight beautiful little skeins of yarn sitting on the floor along with his missing buttons and some toothpicks.

"Hurrah, hurrah! Now I can finish the blanket," cried the weaver.

"And I bet I know who spun this yarn. Come in and let me thank you," he called.

"Next year we can spin wool together."

The weaver quickly finished the yellow blanket and gave it to his friend, who never knew just how many hands and paws had spun the yarn it was woven with.

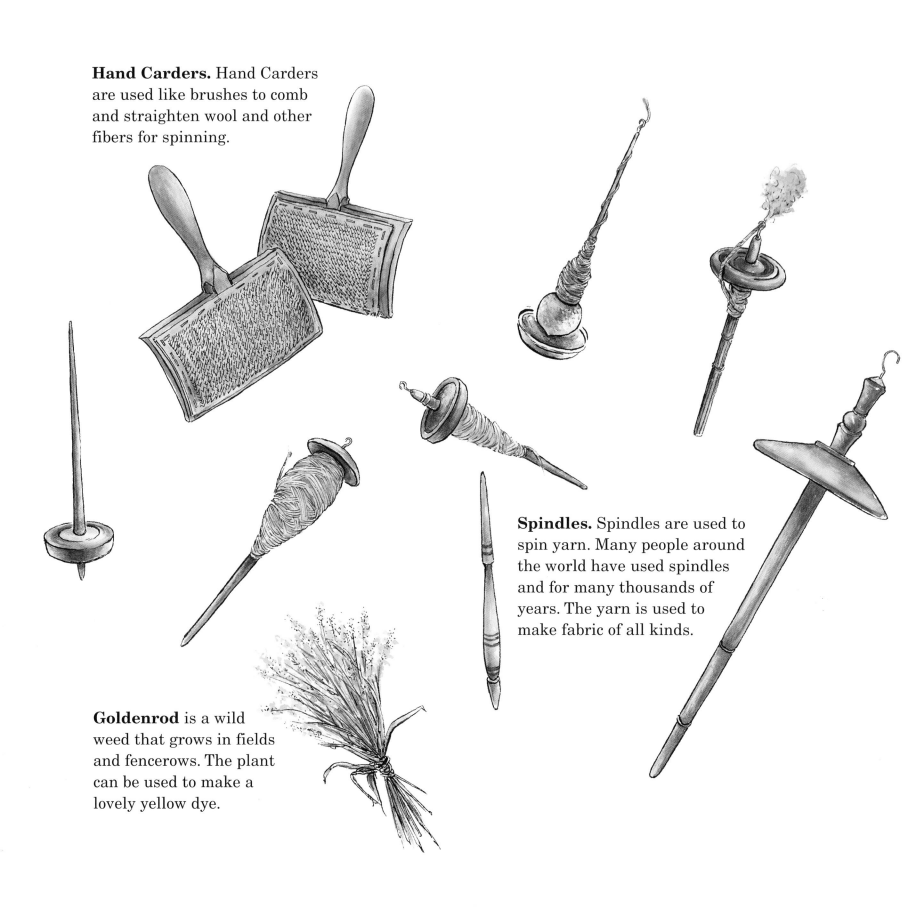

Hand Carders. Hand Carders are used like brushes to comb and straighten wool and other fibers for spinning.

Spindles. Spindles are used to spin yarn. Many people around the world have used spindles and for many thousands of years. The yarn is used to make fabric of all kinds.

Goldenrod is a wild weed that grows in fields and fencerows. The plant can be used to make a lovely yellow dye.